PIT PONY

Joyce Barkhouse

gage EDUCATIONAL PUBLISHING COMPANY
A DIVISION OF CANADA PUBLISHING CORPORATION
TORONTO ONTARIO CANADA

Canadian Cataloguing in Publication Data

Barkhouse, Joyce, 1913-
  Pit pony

(Jeanpac paperback original)
ISBN 0-7715-7023-6

1. Cape Breton Island (N.S.) - History - Juvenile fiction.   2. Ponies - Juvenile fiction.   I. Van Der Linde, Henry.   II. Title.   III. Series: Jean pac paperback original.

PS8553.A75P5 1989   jC813'.54   C89-094543-8
PZ7.B37Pi 1989

Design: Marc Mireault
Cover and illustrations: Henry Van Der Linde

ISBN: 0-7715-7023-6

        7 8 9 WC 97 96

Written, Printed, and Bound in Canada

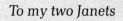

To my two Janets

CHAPTER 1

The wild horse screamed as its feet left the deck of the schooner. Then its body hung, limp and helpless in the sling under its belly, as it was winched ashore.

A crowd had gathered on the wharf to witness the spectacle of wild horses captured on far-off Sable Island, and brought to Nova Scotia to work in the coal mines of Cape Breton.

Among the watchers, a small boy stood with hands clenched into fists, his face twisted with pity. Tears trickled down his pale cheeks. His name was William Maclean but he was known around the coal mining town of Green Bay as "Wee Willie." Sometimes he was called "Wee Willie the Whistler."

Many of the Cape Breton miners had nicknames, like "Danny the Dancer," "Stumpy Sam," and "Freddie the Fiddler." This was because so many of the Scottish families had names exactly the same. There were three William Macleans in

1

Green Bay School, but Wee Willie was the one best known around town. When he wasn't at school he could usually be found hanging around one of the livery stables, wanting to help with the horses.

In those days, back at the beginning of the twentieth century, horses were a part of everyday life. A coal mine could not operate without them. In Willie's town, many different breeds were for hire—fast, pretty Morgans for driving or riding horseback, and big, strong Clydesdales for pulling heavy loads. Pairs of matched white horses were hired for weddings, and blacks for funerals.

Wee Willie loved them all. In fact, when he was with horses he forgot about everything else. Too often, he came home for supper too late to help with the chores. On these occasions, his little sisters, Maggie and Sara, had to go to the town well for water. It was much too hard for them. They staggered home with the heavy tin pail between them, sloshing water against their long skirts. His older sister, Nellie, who had all the other household tasks to do, had to feed the hens, bring in the eggs, and carry in scuttles of coal for the kitchen stove.

Tonight, Willie was late again. Not

until the last horse struggled to its feet on the slippery wharf, did he realize the sun had almost set. He dashed a grubby fist across his eyes and started for home. He knew how angry his father would be. He would give Willie a thrashing and send him to bed without his supper.

Willie didn't mind the thrashing quite as much as he minded going to bed without his supper. The Maclean children, whose mother had died when Willie was six, didn't have as much to eat as some of the other families. His father, Rory Maclean, was a pit miner who worked with Willy's brother, John, in the Ocean Deeps Mine. He was a proud, stern man. He refused to charge at the Company Store. All the same, the family lived in a Company house, for the sake of cheap rent.

Willie lived on Sunny Row. Not a tree nor a flower grew along the dirt lane. The houses were all the same, shaped like rectangles with slanting roofs and square, small-paned windows. It was called Sunny Row because of a habit the men had of sunning themselves during the long afternoons of the brief, Nova Scotia summers. The miners' wives put wooden washtubs on the steps, and here the

3

colliers sat when they came home from the pit, still black around the eyes with coal dust. They would soak their sore, tired feet in the warm water, and joke back and forth while they watched their children play ball or kick the can along the dusty street.

But now it was October. The days were short and the nights were cold. Willie should have been home from school long since.

He went around to the back of the house. As soon as he stepped into the porch he smelled supper. *Ceann groppaig!** His favourite dish! His sister, Nellie, was a good cook. And he would have to go to bed without a single mouthful.

He opened the door a crack and peeked in.

There they were, the whole family, six of them, seated around the table in the warm kitchen. His frowning, dark-mustached father sat at one end. The lamplight shone on the bright red heads of Nellie and his big brother, John, and made pale ovals of the faces of the dark-eyed little ones, Maggie and Sara. It reflected on the spectacles of his tiny old grandmother in her frilled, white cap, as she peered over at him from her rocking

_____
* cown' graw' pik

4

chair. In the middle of the table sat the steaming *ceann groppaig*, a huge codfish head stuffed with a pudding made of rolled oats and flour and mashed cod livers.

All this, Willie saw in the flash of a second—and he was puzzled. What had happened? Usually the children ate first, because there weren't enough chairs to go around. When there was a ceilidh,* or when the minister came to call, then Nellie would borrow extra chairs from one of the neighbours. But tonight there was no guest.

He opened the door a crack wider.

His father glared at him from under his bushy, black eyebrows. "Come in," he ordered. "Shut the door. You're letting in a cold draft."

Willie went in, hanging his head, shamefaced, and shut the door. Then the whole family shouted together, "Happy Birthday!"

He had forgotten. It was October 12, 1902, and he was eleven years old.

"Wash your hands and come to the table for blessing," said his father.

Willie went to the dry sink and poured cold water from a bucket into the tin basin.

* kay′ lee

6

"How could you forget your own birthday?" scolded seven-year-old Sara, the youngest of the family, bouncing up and down in her chair.

"Hush! Bow your head for blessing," said Rory Maclean.

As soon as Willie sat down, his father prayed, "God bless this house and this family. Teach them Thy ways, O Lord. May William learn, from this day on, to assume his full share of family responsibilities. Amen."

He raised his head. The corners of his mustache lifted and he smiled at them all, including Willie. As if a black cloud had floated away and the sun had come out, they all smiled back. Rory Maclean picked up a knife and fork and prepared to serve the *ceann groppaig*. Willie felt a warm and happy glow inside.

"But where were you, Willie? Why were you so late?" Sara persisted.

"Mmm!" Willie savoured his first mouthful. "I was down by the waterfront to see the wild horses come in from Sable Island. Me and some other boys wanted to see them unloading."

"And did you?" asked his big, red-headed brother, John, as he reached for a thick slice of homemade bread.

"We did," said Willie. "And a sad sight it was, too. All them little wild, shaggy horses, scared to death. Some of them was cut and bleeding."

"Why?" asked Sara.

"Because when they're aboard a schooner, they're tied by the legs and head so's they won't fall down or rear up in a storm," explained Willie, between mouthfuls. Then he added, "It's a terrible thing to capture wild horses and make them go down the pits."

"Maybe it won't do," said his father. "Wild horses are apt to be fractious. But the Company can't find enough trained ponies to work the narrow seams."

Sara tossed her blond pigtails. "Why. . . ." she began, but her father interrupted impatiently.

"Be quiet, child, and eat up." He looked over at Willie and frowned. "Willie needs to get home every night for his supper. If he don't, he'll stay little and stunted like a Sable Island pony. He's got to grow up big and strong to be a good miner."

Willie was silent. He didn't want to grow up to be a miner. He wasn't like John who had never thought of being anything else. It had been a proud day for John when he had left school at fourteen and gone off to work with his father. He was considered a man now, with all a man's rights. No more thrashings for a boy who brought home a pay envelope.

Willie looked up at his father. His big, long-lashed brown eyes were troubled. "Maybe I won't be a miner," he muttered.

His father put down his knife and fork.

Everybody stopped eating.

"Not be a miner! What will you be, then?"

Willie was trembling. "I like horses. Maybe I could be a blacksmith...or... something."

"A blacksmith! How could a puny mite like you work at a forge and swing a great hammer?"

Willie hung his dark head, but he muttered, "'Twould be no harder than swingin' a pickaxe diggin' out coal in a mine."

His father's face grew red with anger. "And where would the money come from to buy a shop and set you up with all your fancy ideas? We're a family of colliers, me and my father before me. I never thought to breed a lazy, good-for-nothin' brat who won't even do his share of chores. From now on, you get yourself straight home

9

from school. If you're late for supper just once more, that's the end of school for you. You'll be down in the pits before you know what's happened to you."

The children were silent, afraid of their father's hot temper. Little Maggie, the quiet, gentle one, began to cry. The birthday supper was ruined.

As soon as the dishes were cleared from the table Willie did his lessons, lighted his stub of candle, and crept away upstairs to bed.

Upstairs were two bedrooms and a wide, square hall. Willie and John slept together in a white-painted, iron bedstead in the hall. Now Willie crawled under the patchwork quilts. He blew out his candle, but for a long time he couldn't get to sleep. He was full of fear and anger.

He muttered to himself under his breath, "I'll never go down the mines. Never, never, never. I'm not goin' to live all my life in the black pits and get killed by an explosion, like my grandpa. I'll run away. Maybe I'll get aboard a ship. Maybe I'll live on Sable Island with the wild horses. Nobody could find me there."

He knew a lot about Sable Island, one of the loneliest places in the world. It was fully described in the second chapter of his history book. He thought about it now and imagined he was there, riding free on the back of a wild horse over the sand dunes and through the long grasses, where the waves thundered in crashing white foam on the beaches.

But when he fell asleep, he dreamed of being lost, all alone, in the pitch dark tunnel of a coal mine.

CHAPTER 2

For the next few days Willie got home from school before his father. All the same he couldn't keep away from the Sable Island horses. As soon as school was dismissed, he was first out of the yard. He raced down the dirt road until he came to a path which led through a wood, across an open field, and down a hill to an old, abandoned farm.

Here, just outside the town limits, the horses were being kept in a pasture while they recovered from the rough voyage across the North Atlantic. The healthy, more docile ones were immediately broken to harness.

On his way to visit the horses, Willie passed a wild apple tree. Some fruit still clung to the branches. He filled his pockets with the best he could find. At the pasture gate, he hung over the bars and held out his hand with an apple on his palm. He whistled coaxingly. The horses only lifted their heads and stared at him.

One of the trainers called out, "Hey, you kid! Keep out of the paddock!"

"O.K.!" Willie shouted back. "But I can watch, can't I?"

"Sure. Just stay outside the fence."

Willie couldn't linger long, but the next day, and the next, he was back again. The men, busy tending sores and bruises, or fitting horses to bit and bridle, paid little attention to him.

On the fourth visit, one of the small, shaggy mares responded to his call. She was a chestnut with a long, pale mane and a white blaze on her nose. She trotted up to the gate, stretched out her neck nervously, and ate the apple from his hand.

He gave her another, letting the cold juice mixed with her warm saliva trickle through his fingers. He looked into her brown eyes, and a wonderful, warm feeling flowed through his body. Right then, he knew he loved that horse more than anything. He wanted her for his own.

He looked up to see one of the horse trainers watching him. He recognized Big Mac from one of the livery stables. Big Mac stopped what he was doing and came over to talk to him.

"You're a good one with horses, Wee Willie," he said, "but you needn't think you're working magic. That there mare's already been trained. She belonged to the lighthouse keeper's family. They called her 'Gem.' "

Willie stared in astonishment. "Honest? She's not a wild horse?"

Big Mac spit out a stream of tobacco juice. "Well, she was wild once, a'course. But horses are often caught and broke to the saddle on the Island. They're used to patrol the shores in case of shipwreck."

Willie patted the mare's neck. "Gem," he murmured. He rubbed her velvety nose, then he looked up at Big Mac. "Do you think she'd let me ride her?"

Big Mac's grin vanished. "Hey! Don't you dare try any tricks like that. If she threw you, it might scare the other horses. Just you keep out of this paddock, Wee Willie."

"O.K.," said Willie.

But he couldn't get the idea out of his head.

The next day, which was Thursday, Gem came trotting toward him as soon as she heard his whistle. He had saved a piece of molasses cookie from his lunch for her. He talked to her for a long time and rubbed her nose.

He was almost late for supper.

* * * * *

On Friday afternoon, when Gem was nibbling a lump of sugar from his hand, Willie noticed that all the men had gone home. It had been a dark, drizzly day. Willie looked all around cautiously, but not a person was in sight.

"This is my chance," he thought.

His heart began to thump with excitement.

"Come on, Gem," he coaxed.

He felt in his pocket for the last sticky crumbs of sugar. He held out his hand and kept moving backward until the mare was standing sideways to the gate. She stretched out her neck over the bars, and lifted her upper lip for the treat.

Willie scrambled to the top bar and jumped. As he did so, the bar snapped under his weight with a loud crack. He landed astride the mare's back with a thump.

With a loud whinny of fright, Gem reared and bucked. Willie caught her long, tangled mane in his hands and hung on. Gem galloped off in a wide circle. As she came around to the gate with the broken bar, she gathered her legs beneath her and jumped.

Willie fell to the ground. For a moment he lay half-stunned. Then he scrambled to his feet.

Too late!

He could hear the thud of Gem's hooves fading away into the distance.

He stood frozen. The horses in the paddock snorted and stamped their hooves. They could escape, too! Instantly, Willie came alive. He pulled out the bottom bar and placed it on top.

He ran up the hill, across the open field, and into the woods where Gem had disappeared. He could see her tracks in the soft soil of the path. He stopped and whistled a long, shrill call.

Nothing happened.

It was very still inside the wood. A bluejay called, "Thief! Thief!" A sob caught in his throat. Where was that horse? He ran on, following her tracks.

The path ended, and he came out on the road. Here, there were so many horse droppings and hoofprints, it was impossible to pick out Gem's tracks. Still Willie ran on, into country where he had seldom been before. On either side of the road were rocks and stunted spruce trees, with here and there patches of barren, boggy soil covered with brown reeds and grasses.

He was out of breath and panting. Every little while, he stopped to whistle and call, "Gem! Gem! Come, Gem!"

His head hurt. He put up a hand under his grey, woollen cap and felt a lump as big as an egg. He must have landed on a rock when he fell from Gem's back.

It began to rain. Soon, it would be really dark. In the distance came the shrill sound of the siren at the colliery. The end of the shift! His father would be starting for home.

Willie stopped running and stood still. "Even if I turn back and run all the way, I can never get home first!"

He had said the words out loud but there was no one to hear. He felt hopeless and helpless. What could he do? Should he go back and not tell anybody what had happened? Maybe the stablemen would think Gem had escaped by herself. Anyway, maybe he wouldn't try to find Gem. Maybe the little mare was happy running free. Gem could find shelter in the woods from the storms of winter. But what about food? On Sable Island, it was said that the fierce winds swept the snow away from the tall grasses, but in Nova Scotia, sometimes the snow piled up as high as the eaves on the houses.

Willie walked slowly on. He didn't know what to do. Maybe Gem would be all right, but what about himself, Willie Maclean? His father would be furious if Willie told the truth about how he had tried to ride Gem, and how she had jumped the broken gate. If Willie refused to say what happened, he would be even more furious.

"Pa never goes back on his word. He's going to take me out of school and make me go down the pits," Willie muttered to himself.

"If Mama was alive she wouldn't let him do this to me. She wouldn't!"

He tried to remember what his mother looked like but it was five years now since she had died, in pain, of some terrible disease. He could hardly remember her pale face, framed in red hair, but he could remember her smile. He remembered how she had looked at him with love and pride in her blue eyes.

"You may not grow up to be a big man, Willie," she had said once, "but you have lots of brains. You study hard at school and you can be...well, you can be

19

whatever you want to be."

He always treasured those words in his heart. His mother had loved and protected him.... Well, Nellie loved him, too, but she never stood up for him against their father. Nellie was scared. She liked things to be quiet and peaceful. Tears mixed with the rain beating against Willie's face. A sharp gust of wind blew his cap off. It went rolling ahead of him and stopped in a puddle. As he picked it up, he cried out loud, "What can I do?"

It was dark. He could hardly see the road. He looked up and saw a speck of light not far ahead. It was the first house he had seen for a long time. What would the folks say if he knocked at the door and said, "Please let me in."

They would ask many questions. Questions he didn't want to answer. No, he dared not knock on the door...but as he came closer he saw the shape of a barn. His heart gave a little leap of hope. He could hide in the barn and sleep there all night. In the morning, he could decide what to do.

He was in luck. The barn door was not locked.

A cow greeted him with a soft moo

when he stepped inside. A horse whinnied. It was very dark in the barn, but it smelled of hay and good animal smells. It was warm, and dry, and safe.

He closed the door carefully and felt around until he found a pile of hay. He stripped off his damp jacket and cap, pulled off his wet boots, and burrowed deep into the scratchy, sweet-smelling mow.

He was almost asleep when he heard something rustling in the hay. A wet nose touched his face. Soft fur rubbed against his cheek and a loud purr sounded in his ear.

"Hi, puss," he whispered, smiling to himself.

The cat snuggled warmly beside him. In a few moments, they were both sound asleep.

CHAPTER 3

Willie didn't hear the farmer come into the barn in the morning. He awoke with a start when a pitchfork, thrust into the haymow, narrowly escaped his head.

"Hey!" he shouted.

He pawed his way out, and the cat came after him. Then he and the farmer stood and stared at each other. The farmer was quite old, with a flowing white beard and long white hair. He spoke first.

"Well, now," he drawled, "I never thought to find a brownie in my barn."

Willie, who had heard stories of brownies and elves from his grandmother, brushed the hay out of his eyes.

"Oh, sir, I'm not a brownie," he laughed.

"Who be ye, then?" demanded the old man.

"I'm Willie...I'm William...uh...just William."

"Well, then, Just William, what are you doin' in my haymow at the break of day?"

Willie was silent, trying to think what he should say. He heard the roosters crowing loudly outside. The cow mooed anxiously, asking to be milked. Willie scuffed his feet on the rough floor and hung his head.

"I...I...my horse ran away," he stammered. "I ran after her and got caught in the dark and the rain, so I took shelter in your barn. I hope you don't mind, sir."

The old man looked him over. His eyes were very blue and sharp under his white eyebrows. "A bit young to be ownin' a horse, ain't ya? What's your father's name?"

Willie turned and began digging in the hay for his boots. "I won't be botherin' you any longer," he mumbled.

The farmer picked up a tin pail. "Just a minute. Maybe you are a brownie, after all. I'll give ye a sup of milk, along with puss."

Willie realized then he was very hungry.

"Oh, thank you, sir. I'll clean out your stables and curry your horses...and whatever else you want me to do," he offered.

The old man said no more. He picked up a low, three-legged stool and set about milking his cow. "Swish, swish...swish, swish," the rhythmic sound of the milking set Willie to whistling. He looked doubtfully at his damp jacket and decided to spread it out on the hay to dry. He didn't want to catch his "death of cold," as his grandma always said he would, if he didn't change into dry things.

The farmer rinsed the cat's dish out in a bucket of water before he filled it with warm milk, and handed it to Willie. Oh, how good it tasted! Willie did not often have milk at home, because it cost too much.

He didn't mind mucking out. He had often done it before. He knew how to use a curry comb, too.

The black mare had a sway back, and wheezed when she breathed.

"I hope she's not got the heaves, sir," said Willie, anxiously.

The farmer smiled. "Her name is Topsy, and you can call me Charley," he said. "We're both gettin' old, that's for sure. In the spring, I'll have to buy a young colt. I like to break and train my own horses."

He inspected the clean stables, and watched Willie using brush and curry comb.

"You're doin' a good job, William," he praised him. "I guess you've been around horses before. At first I thought you might be a runaway from the mines—a collier's son."

Willie's hand stopped, and he felt his face turn red. "I...I really was tryin' to catch a horse," he said.

"Hmmm," said Charley. "I doubt if you can find that horse, now. Usually a runaway will find its own way home after it gets over a fright. It's probably back in its own stable, right now."

"But Gem doesn't have a stable!" cried Willie, without thinking.

Charley pulled at his long, white beard. "Never heard of a horse without a stable," he said. "Except maybe a wild horse, but we don't have wild horses in Cape Breton."

Willie was silent.

Then Charley said, "Tell you what. I can give a day's work before you go back to where you came from. I need help harvestin' the rest of my turnips before the ground freezes. It looks to be a nice, sunny day."

He picked up his pail of milk and started for the barn door.

"Keep out of sight of the house. I can't

ask you inside because my sister keeps house for me. She's as cranky as a mother bear in spring. Bide here until I get back."

Willie busied himself around the barn until Charley returned, bringing an old grey sweater with a thick slice of freshly baked bread wrapped up inside. He smiled at Willie, a twinkle in his bright blue eyes. Willie smiled back, and then they both laughed aloud as Charley slipped the sweater over Willie's head.

It was much too big. The waistband hung below his knees, and he had to roll the sleeves back six times before his hands were free. But it was warm and clean and sweet-smelling, and the bread tasted even better than the bread his grandmother baked at home.

Charley handed him a shovel and picked up the handles of a wooden wheelbarrow.

"Come along, then," he ordered, and they set off side by side for the turnip field.

Wee Willie Maclean, who had hardly ever been outside the drab colliery town of Green Bay, thought old Charley's farm must be the most beautiful place on earth. He forgot his troubles. He whistled softly as they tramped across a small pasture carpeted with green grass. Ahead, a stand of maples and birches glowed red and yellow and orange, dressed in bright autumn colours.

The path to the vegetable garden led through the wood. Inside, the sunlight streamed through the branches, and touched upon open mossy glades with gold. Willie stopped to gaze around him in wonder. Charley stopped, too. It was so still and quiet, Willie could hear small creatures rustling through the undergrowth. Maybe rabbits, he thought.

Charley started on again, wheelbarrow creaking. Willie followed. They came to a small stream, half-hidden by brown rushes and green bracken, gurgling over mossy stones. They crossed a narrow footbridge of old planks and came out into bright sunshine again.

Now they were in the turnip field. Willie set to work. It didn't take long to fill the barrow. Charley picked up the handles.

"You keep on digging, lad. Put the turnips in neat piles. I'll be the carrier and take them back and store them in the barn."

Willie worked hard all morning. Charley went back and forth to the barn, storing the turnips for the winter. At noon, he came back with a small box.

"Here's some lunch for ye, lad. Take a break and I'll be back after I have a bite and my afternoon nap."

All the time Willie had been working, he had tried not to think about what might have happened to Gem or about what he should do next. Now, as he perched on a big rock at the edge of the field and munched on the bread and cheese Charley had brought, he tried to make a plan. He had no idea in which direction Gem had travelled, so how could he continue to hunt for her?

He loved the farm. He wished he could stay and work for Charley forever. He choked on the last bite of bread, and put the oatmeal cookie in the pocket of the old sweater. He was no longer hungry, but he was thirsty. He decided to go back to the brook to wash his face and hands, and get a drink.

He went back whistling a sad, Scottish ditty. He felt as if he was all alone in the beautiful autumn world, breathing its sweet, cool air, but as he bent over the gurgling stream to drink of the crystal-clear water, he heard something move in the bushes.

He waited, listening.

He had a feeling that he was being watched. He looked up, and there amongst the shadowy trees, sunlight flecking her shaggy chestnut coat, was Gem.

Willie remained very still, afraid if he moved he might startle her.

But Gem knew him.

She gave a soft whicker in greeting. Willie felt in his pocket for the cookie and held it out on his hand. Gem stepped through the shallow brook and came to nibble. The young boy put his cheek against her warm, soft neck and put up a hand to brush the rough, tangled mane out of her eyes.

"Oh, Gem, Gem," he whispered.

CHAPTER 4

When Charley came back, he found them there by the brook. He stood for a few moments, silently watching the boy with his arms around the neck of the shaggy horse. Then he spoke softly.

"Will she follow you, lad? If so, we can put her in the barnyard pasture for the time being."

Willie nodded. Holding Gem's mane, he made soft, coaxing noises. Obediently, the mare plodded after him until they came to the fenced area behind the barn. Willie didn't want to leave her there alone, but Charley said, "Now we'll go back and get the rest of the turnips."

By mid-afternoon, the turnips were harvested. When he came back for the last barrow load, Charley said, "Let's you and me sit over on the big rock. We better have a heart-to-heart talk, William."

Willie's heart sank. He didn't want to have a heart-to-heart talk. But Charley wasted no time. He picked up a long stalk of grass and chewed on it as he talked.

"That's an odd-lookin' mare you've got there, lad, with her short legs and round, fat belly. I never saw a horse with such a thick pelt. I've heard tell that's the size and shape of a Sable Island horse. But a'course, this one don't seem very wild. If it wasn't for that, I'd make a guess she's one of the shipment I heard came from the Island to work in the coal mines at Green Bay."

Willie hung his head. He couldn't lie to the kind old farmer.

"You're right," he mumbled, "Gem is a Sable Island horse. She's not wild because she used to belong to a lighthouse keeper."

Charley put a hand on Willie's shoulder. "That explains a lot," he said, "but it don't explain how come you own her."

Willie felt tears sting his eyes. He dashed them away with his fists. He made up his mind to tell Charlie the whole truth about what had happened. And he did. Then he told how angry his father would be.

"I don't want to go home," said Willie. "I don't want to go down into the pits when I'm eleven years old. And I don't want Gem to go down, either. I'd rather go down myself than have Gem go down. Maybe...could you buy her, Charley?"

Charley shook his head. "'Fraid not, lad. I like to train my own horses. This one has run away once and she might run away again. She's not used to farm work."

"She's not used to mine work, either," said Willie. He felt as if his heart would break.

"I'm sorry," said Charley. He threw away the straw and combed his fingers through his white beard. "You and I have to face up to facts, lad. My farm lies only two kilometres outside the town of Green Bay. It won't be long before someone comes lookin' for that horse—and like as not someone will come lookin' for you. If they find that mare in my barnyard and you in my barn, and I haven't reported either of you, I could be accused of kidnapping. I'll end up in jail."

"Oh, no!" cried Willie.

"That's the way it is," said Charley firmly. "Now you'll have to decide what to do. You can keep on runnin' and hidin' until you get caught. Or you can go home now and 'fess up to the truth."

Willie's face turned very white. He felt sick inside. But he had decided.

All he said was, "How'll I take Gem back?"

"You can lead her. I'll make a halter out

of a piece of rope and a strip of leather. You can fill your pockets with oats and coax her along," Charley suggested.

Willie got up from the rock. "I'd better get home before dark," he said.

The evening shadows grew long as Willie and Gem trudged along the highway. They met only a few people along the way. Two ladies in a rubber-tired buggy with a bony, black horse, stopped gossiping long enough to stare at the small boy leading the queer little horse. A farmer on foot, tipped his cap and said, "Good evening," without stopping.

By the time Willie and Gem plodded up the last hill, the sun had set, and the sky blazed red behind the black buildings and the great bull-wheel at the pithead. Willie didn't want to look at that dark scene. He didn't want to think about those black tunnels under the earth that reached far out under the Atlantic Ocean. He didn't want to think about the pits, but he couldn't help it.

Suddenly his thoughts were interrupted. Gem had caught a whiff of the horses penned in the paddock down by the waterfront. With a whicker of joy, she reared up on her hind legs and almost broke away from Willie. He shouted at her and hung on for dear life. She took off at a half-gallop, dragging him along beside her. Somehow, he managed to stay on his feet and guide her to the fence. He took down the bars, and off she galloped across the grass to join the others, still wearing her make-shift halter and rope.

Willie replaced the bars and leaned over the fence to watch her.

Poor little Gem! She was happy now. She did not know of the sad fate that awaited her.

With a heavy heart, Willie turned away and slowly started for home.

As soon as he came to Sunny Row, he knew something had happened. People were standing about in small groups, talking in low voices as they did after an accident in the coal mine. Some of the people looked up and nodded, but nobody smiled or said, "Hello."

Then he saw a black wreath hung on the door of one of the houses. Somebody was dead. That was where Ed MacNeil, his father's buddy, lived.

For as long as Willie could remember, these two men had walked to the mine together and had worked side by side. They were hand-pick miners, who got paid for however much coal they got out

in a day. It was said that the pair were the fastest and best workers in the colliery. It would be a terrible thing for Willie's father if Ed MacNeil had been killed.

People were gathered on his own front doorstep, too. Willie's heart gave a thump. He was afraid to ask questions. He went around to the back and opened the door into the kitchen. The table was covered with goodies—an apple pie, a loaf of brown bread, a plate of cookies. It looked as if the neighbours had brought the party food as if for a ceilidh—or for a death....

Everything was quiet. Willie looked around the room. His grandmother sat in her usual chair, rocking back and forth, her hands idle. The chair made rhythmic, squeaking sounds. Where were the children?

The door to the parlour stood open. A smell of creolin, the antiseptic that was used if anyone had a cut or wound, almost drowned out the spicy odour of the food on the table.

"What's wrong, Grandma?" Willie whispered, but his grandmother seemed not to hear him. She continued to rock back and forth, back and forth. Nellie came out of the parlour and closed the door softly behind her. Her red hair hung in strings about her pale face, and her eyes were red and swollen from weeping.

"Nellie! What happened?" cried Willie.

"Shh! There's been an accident, a rock fall in the mine. Mr. MacNeil was killed and Papa...Papa's in the infirmary. He's been hurt. He's been hurt bad."

For a moment, Willie couldn't speak. Then, "Where's John?" he whispered.

Nellie nodded toward the parlour door. "In there. He's got cuts and bruises and a broken leg, but he'll be all right. It's Papa...." Nellie sank down on a chair and sobbed aloud. "Oh, Willie! Where have you been? All this time...I thought you might be dead, too."

Willie put his arm around her awkwardly. He could think of nothing to say except, "I'm sorry! I'm sorry!"

He couldn't tell her now about how he had let Gem run away. He couldn't tell her about how happy he had been on the farm—while all the time such terrible things had been happening at home.

His mind raced. He knew the Company wouldn't let them stay in the house a single day if it was known that there wasn't a wage earner in the family. The winter before, he had seen Mrs. Wilson with her five little children, wandering the streets, and he had seen the pitiful shack she had tried to build out of pieces of carpet and scraps of lumber. He knew two of her babies had died of cold and hunger. He didn't know what had become of the rest of them.

He spoke in a very loud voice. "No, we won't be out on the street. Pa was going to send me down the mine anyways. I'll go down...tomorrow."

Nellie stared at him through her tears.

"Lots of kids go to work when they're eleven," said Willie, in the same strange, loud voice.

Nellie said, "Oh, Willie, if you could! Just until John gets better."

"And Papa, too," said Willie.

Nellie pushed back strands of her red hair. "You better wash up. I'll get you something to eat," she said.

The rest of the evening would remain forever a blur in Willie's mind. He ate his meal without really tasting anything. The little girls were brought home by the neighbours and put to bed. The doctor dropped in to see John. After he left, Willie was allowed to go into the parlour to talk to his brother for a few minutes.

"Don't worry, John. I'm goin' down

tomorrow. There'll still be a wage earner in this family," he told him.

"Good," said John, drowsily. "Pa would be proud. Wish't I could show you around. You'll start out as a trapper, you know."

"I know," said Willie. "Can I borrow your piece-can to carry my lunch?"

"Sure. Take whatever you need."

The doctor had given John a painkiller, drops of morphine and chloroform on a spoonful of sugar. His voice was getting thick and his eyelids closed.

"Keep whistlin', Willie," he murmured, and tried to smile.

CHAPTER 5

That night Willie's dreams were not of school or wild horses, but of broken bodies and blood on the coal. Before dawn, Nellie awakened him, bringing a lighted candle.

"Come down and get dressed where it's warm, by the kitchen stove. I've got some of John's pit clothes ready for you."

Willie moved as if he was still dreaming. John's sweater, like old Charley's, was much too big for him. Nellie pinned it together at the neck with safety pins. Willie rolled up the legs of the overalls.

He ate as much as he could of the hot oatmeal porridge, while Nellie filled a container with water. She added half a handful of raw oatmeal and a few drops of molasses. This would help with the dry taste of coal dust in his mouth. He was too young to chew tobacco, as the adult miners did.

It was time to go. Willie hesitated. "I wish't I had a buddy. I wish't I didn't have to go alone."

Nellie's eyes were full of pity. "I'd like to walk over with you, Willie. But you know how superstitious miners are. If they meet a woman when they're going to work in the mornin', they think it's terrible bad luck. Most of them would turn back. Anyway, you're sure of a job. The doctor spoke for you."

Willie picked up his two cans. "I know. Goodbye, Nellie."

It was very dark outside at that hour of the morning. After Willie left the Row, there was not even the comfort of a dimly lighted window. He could hear the crunch, crunch of feet and the low voices of the other men on the road, all walking toward the pithead.

Willie began to whistle softly to himself to keep up his courage. A shadowy shape came up beside him.

"Is that you, Wee Willie?"

"Yes."

"I heard you was goin' down. I heard your father was hurt bad."

"Yes, he was hurt. John, too."

Willie recognized the voice of an older boy, Simon Ross, who had been in his class at school. Simon was a bully. Willie had been afraid of him. He was glad when Simon had left school to work in the mine.

Now, in the dark and the loneliness he sounded different, almost friendly.

"If I'd known you was goin' down I would've called for you. Are you sure you'll get a job?"

"Yes. The doctor spoke for me. I'll be a trapper."

"Oh. That's what I am, a trapper. You know how to do the work, Willie? You know what a trapper boy does?"

"Yes. He opens and shuts a door to let horses and people go through."

"Well, them doors are called traps because they trap air," said Simon, importantly. "They're part of the ventilation system in the mine. Good air has to be pumped in all the time and bad air has to be pumped out. It's a 'portant job, Willie, bein' a trapper. If you leave one of them traps open, poison gas could collect. A lot of men could die. You could die, too, Willie."

Simon hadn't changed much, after all. He was still trying to scare.

"Yeah, I know all about that, Si," said Willie.

"You have to trap all alone, Willie. It's black dark down there. It's a 'portant job, Willie. Every man's life depends on the life of another in the pits. If the pipe fitters don't fit the pipes right, the mines could be flooded with water. You could drown, Willie. If the pit-prop men don't brace up the ceiling right, you could get killed by a rock fall."

Willie smiled to himself in the dark. Simon had been a stupid boy in school and often had to wear a dunce cap. Behind his back, the kids called him "Simple Simon." But he tormented little kids. He called Willie "teacher's pet" just because Willie always knew his lessons and was at the head of his class. Now Simon wanted to show off how much he had learned about coal mining.

As they neared the pithead, the noise of locomotives which carried the coal to Louisbourg became deafening. Whistles shrieked, bells clanged, cars shunted, wheels rattled, jets of escaping steam hissed, and men shouted. All this noisy action was dimly lit by lanterns hung on posts. The polluted air stung Willie's nose and eyes.

It was a relief to step inside the lamp house. Here, men exchanged their metal tags for the "clanny lamps" which would be their only light once they were underground. Dozens of men were milling about. The big room was filled with the hum of their loud conversations. Willie felt dazed and bewildered.

Simon took him by the shoulder. "Come on. We'll find One Arm Joe. He'll give you a tag and lamp."

Simon was full of confidence. He was eager to show Willie around.

"That tag is very 'portant. It's got your number on it, see? When it's on the hook here, it tells the manager you're down in the mine."

"Yes," said Willie. "That's in case of an explosion or a fire or a cave in."

"Yeah. When you get back from work, you give Joe your lantern and he'll give you your tag. Tomorrow, you trade again."

It was time to go. The boys walked together down a slope until they came to the deputy's cabin, a small underground building. Here, each miner was told if his workplace was safe on that day. It had to be free from a dangerous level of fire-damp, the poisonous and explosive gas which seeped out from the displaced coal.

An overseer checked daily to see if it was safe. Sometimes, he took a live canary in a cage. If the bird got sick and toppled from its perch, that shaft was closed until it checked safe. Sometimes the overseer took his safety lamp and held it high over his head. He could tell if the level of the gas was dangerous by the colour of the halo of light which formed above the flame.

Today, both boys were told their workplaces were safe.

"Now, we'll get on the next rake. You know—the string of cars that run on rails. It'll take us down the slope. When we get to your landing, I'll tell ya. You'll have to walk from there," said Simon.

Willie jumped into a box car when the rake ground to a stop. He crouched down between men who were jammed together so tightly, Willie could hardly breathe. GRIND. RATTLE. ROAR. The noise was deafening in the confined space. Willie made himself as small as he could and shut his eyes.

Several times the rake ground to a halt, and men got off. Finally, it was Willie's turn.

"Jump off! Level Five!" Simon shouted in his ear.

Willie jumped, and then looked about him in the semi-darkness. Several lanterns hung on nails driven into wooden posts. Behind them, walls of black coal glittered.

"Come on," said Simon. "I'll take ya,

but we gotta hurry. The other boys have to wait till we get there for our shifts."

He started off at a half-trot, stooping slightly to avoid hitting his head on the low ceiling with its protruding, jagged pieces of rock. Willie followed. Being small, he didn't have to duck under low-hanging girders. Underfoot, it was rough going. Thick dust choked his throat in some places. In others, he had to wade through puddles of black water. It was like walking along a narrow railway track. The rails were for boxes of coal, hauled by horses. Every once in a while, Willie could see a moving light in the distance. Then Simon would stop and press his body against the wall to make way for a horse and driver bringing out a load of coal. Finally, they came to a thick wooden door.

"You're late," said a boy's voice.

Simon said, "This here is Willie Maclean."

"Right 'nough. You git here earlier tomorrow," said the other boy, as he picked up his piece-can and left.

Simon kept on giving instructions. "You sit on the headway, see? On the high side of the trap. See that rope? It's a pulley and there's a weight on the end. Pull on the rope to open the door. Hang on, and when the team's safe through, let go. It'll shut itself. Think you can remember that?"

Willie was tired of Simon's silly directions. "I know all that," he said, impatiently.

Simon's voice changed. "Oh, you know everything, don't you? You stuck-up know-it-all," he sneered.

"Well, anyway, thanks for bringing me here," said Willie.

Simon picked up a handful of dirt and flung it in Willie's face. By the time Willie had rubbed the dirt out of his eyes, Simon was gone. He was alone in the eerie dark, lighted only by the tiny flame from his lamp. He wished he hadn't said anything to make Simon mad.

Somewhere, he could hear water dripping. He knew all mines would flood if water wasn't constantly pumped out. He remembered he was actually sitting under the Atlantic Ocean. This was called the "Ocean Deeps" colliery. How could the layers of rock and earth above him support an ocean of water?

Very shortly, he heard the distant clop, clop of horses' hooves and then the creaking wheels of an approaching box. How soon should he open the door? Better open it now, and be sure.

At first, all he could see was a tiny, bobbing light and then, gradually, the shape of a white horse. Over its head it wore a cap and a sort of mask of heavy, decorated leather which fitted between its ears and down over its nose. Around its neck was a heavy, double horse collar, and to this were attached chains which fitted over the short, wooden shafts of the cart. Perched on top of the load of coal, feet astride and braced on the shafts, sat the driver, face smudged with coal dust. He gave Willie a big grin, his teeth shining white in his dirty face.

"Hello, young 'un. How's it goin'?" he greeted.

Willie smiled back. "I just started," he said.

"What's your name?"

"Willie Maclean."

"Oh, you're Rory Maclean's boy."

"Yes," said Willie.

"I'm sorry, real sorry, about the accident."

The driver passed through the trap door and was gone. Willie listened until the sound of the horses' hooves faded into the distance.

It was the longest day of his life. Occasionally he heard men approaching on foot, some carrying lumber, poles, and beams which were used as pit props. These braced ceilings against a rock fall such as the one that had hurt his father and John, and killed his father's buddy. Once a man came through alone carrying a tool box. He was a pipe fitter, come to check on the pipes along which the water flowed as it was pumped out of the mine.

But mostly Willie was alone, waiting, waiting, with nothing to do in the lonely dark. Sometimes, he thought he heard soft scratchings and rustlings which reminded him of the cat in Charley's haymow. Sometimes he whistled softly to himself, tunes his grandmother had taught him, sad Gaelic songs of people drowned at sea, of unfaithful lovers, of people longing for Scotland, the homeland they would never see again. And sometimes he recited lessons to himself. Then he thought of his mother, and of how she had said he could be anything he wanted to be, if only he studied hard. But she didn't know the day would come when he couldn't go to school. She didn't know he wouldn't have a choice, after all.

He tried not to think about his father

lying in the infirmary. He tried not to think about how long he might have to work in the mine. But he couldn't help thinking about Gem. He wondered if the little mare was already down in the mine. She would be more frightened than he was. She wouldn't be able to understand where she was or what was expected of her. He thought how different she was from the big, white horse called Sparky.

The driver was friendly, and that helped. Each time he passed through he would say a few words. Willie learned his name was Ned Hall.

Time dragged. It seemed to Willie he must have been at the trap for many hours when he asked Ned, "What time is it?"

The driver pulled out a watch on a chain. "It's goin' on for ten o'clock."

Only ten! "Oh, I thought it must be noon...I'm hungry."

Ned grinned. "You can eat whenever you want, Willie. But mind the rats."

"The rats?"

"Yeah. There's hundreds of 'em down here. Very tame. When you eat a piece of bread or cheese, hold onto it by one corner. Your hands are black with coal dust, see, and it don't taste so good. Hold

your food by one corner and eat all but that. Give the black pieces to the rats. Giddap, Sparky."

Willie had forgotten about the rats. That accounted for some of the scratchings and rustlings he had heard. Sure enough, as soon as he opened his lunch the rats appeared, maybe a dozen of them. Their eyes glinted yellow and red as they waited.

He didn't mind them. His father had told him rats in a mine served a useful purpose. They fed on bits of hay and spilled grain. Rats could detect the smell of methane gas or firedamp, long before a miner could. So if the men saw a number of rats scurrying through a tunnel they would grab their tools and leave.

Every once in a while, Willie could hear a distant bang followed by a rumble. Another shot of dynamite had been fired to loosen the coal. Each time a shot was fired, there was the danger that a pocket of poisonous gas might escape—the same gas that caused many fatal explosions.

No one was allowed to carry a match into the mine. Nearly all the colliers chewed tobacco since they were not allowed to smoke. Tobacco kept their saliva flowing so their mouths wouldn't become unbearably dry from coal dust. Willie took little sips every now and then from his water can. When he ate his apple, he saved the core.

The next time Ned came through he asked if he could give it to Sparky.

"Sure," said Ned. "Do you like horses?"

"Yes, I do," said Willie.

"Me, too," said Ned. "I've got the best job in the mine."

"That's what I'd like to be—a driver," said Willie, enthusiastically. For the moment he had forgotten how much he hated working underground.

"Good for you," said Ned as he drove on.

Willie thought afterwards he could never have lived through that long, first day in the mine if it hadn't been for Ned Hall. When at last the other trapper boy came to take over, he was so tired he could hardly speak. Later, when he stood amongst the men lining up to turn in their lamps, he caught sight of the round, pale-eyed face of Simon Ross standing by the exit. What was he waiting for?

Willie was scared. "I bet he's going to try to get me on the way home," he thought.

Then he recognized the burly back of the man just ahead of him in the line-up. Fear made him bold.

"Mr. Sutherland, may I walk home with you?" he asked eagerly.

The man turned around and glanced down. "Sure thing, Willie," he said, and continued his conversation with the other man.

As they went out the door, Simon gave Willie a hard look. Willie pretended not to see him.

It was dark outside. He remembered his father saying that sometimes he had worked for months and never seen the light of day. Willie breathed deeply. The frosty air was clean and sweet. Stars twinkled overhead. The world felt wide and free and wonderful.

"This is what a horse must feel like when it gets out of its barn and runs free in the pasture," thought Willie. "No wonder it gallops up and down, and tosses its heels like crazy."

He was too tired to do that. And anyway, Simon was lurking somewhere near.

Willie trudged along close behind Mr. Sutherland.

CHAPTER 6

Nellie met him at the backdoor of the house on Sunny Row.

"Take your pit clothes off here. I'll shake the dust out of them. I've put a tub of hot water in the pantry, behind the curtain, like I do for Pa and John. Give yourself a good wash and I'll come in and scrub your back."

Willie blinked in the light from the kitchen lamp. Everything looked strange and yet familiar, as if in a dream. There was a warm, spicy smell of gingerbread. He felt as if he had been away for a thousand years.

His grandmother smiled at him from her rocking chair beside the black iron stove. The little girls stared at him, wide eyed, from their places at the table, as John came hobbling out of the parlour on crutches.

"How did it go, Willie?" he asked.

"Fine," said Willie.

He was too tired to say anything more. The hot bath and clean clothes made him feel better. So did the news that his father had regained consciousness.

"The doctor told him you've gone to work. He knows," said Nellie.

Tears suddenly smarted Willie's eyes. "Is he gonna get better?" he asked.

"Yes, the doctor thinks so. But it will be a long time before he can work."

"Can you stick it out until this leg gets better? Maybe six weeks or so?" John asked.

"Sure," said Willie, but his heart felt like lead. He didn't want to go back, even for one more day. He wondered what his classmates were doing at school. Did they miss him? Who was at the head of the spelling class now?

Nellie gave him a plate of steaming baked beans, and then Sara burst out, "Guess what, Willie? A man came looking for you. He had a long, white beard like Santa Claus."

"And he brought a bag. I thought it might be full of toys, but it was full of vegetables. Turnips and cabbages and parsnips," Maggie giggled.

Nellie said, "That's *better* than toys. We'll have a real Christmas dinner now."

John laughed. "He said he owed you for some work you did."

Willie was astonished. "That must have been Charley! How did he find out where I live?"

"He knew all about you," said Sara, jumping up and down with excitement so that her pigtails bounced. "He knew Papa had had a bad accident."

"And he knows you're crazy about horses," added Maggie. "But he sure was surprised to know you had gone to the pits to work."

"He kept saying, 'Dear me! Dear me!' over and over," Sara giggled.

John shook his head at his excited little sisters. "What's the mystery, Willie? Was that where you were? At Charley Howe's farm the night you disappeared?"

Willie nodded. He didn't want to talk about it.

His grandmother seldom interfered, but now she said, in her crackly voice, "That's enough, bairns. Leave Willie alone. He's tired."

"Two more days of work, then you get Sunday off," said John. "You can tell us about your adventures then."

The next morning before Willie had finished eating his porridge, Simon Ross was at the door. Willie looked up with a frown.

"You go along. You don't need to wait for me," he said, angrily.

"It's no bother," said Simon, grinning at him.

"I know my way," Willie insisted.

"I'll wait for ya," said Simon.

Nellie watched from the kitchen stove. She looked worried, but she didn't say anything.

Willie gulped down the last spoonful of his porridge and picked up his piece-can.

"'Bye, Nellie," he said.

Outside, a half-moon was still shining in the starry sky. Willie tried to keep away from Simon, but the bigger boy kept brushing up against him. Once, when Willie bent to tie his bootlace, a nudge from behind sent him sprawling on his face.

"Oops! Sorry!" said Simon. He helped him to his feet as two men passed them talking earnestly to each other. Willie tried to run and catch up with them, but Simon blocked his way.

All this time they had not said anything to each other. Now Simon said, "Why don't that red-headed sister of yours have no boyfriends?"

Willie was silent.

"I guess she's too ugly. All them freck-les," said Simon.

Willie's face grew hot with anger. He knew why Nellie didn't have a boyfriend. Rory Maclean was a very strict father. He would hardly ever let Nellie go to a ceilidh, and whenever a lad came to call, he would glower at him under his black brows. The boy would grow more and more uneasy and leave early, not to come back.

Secretly, Willie was glad. He didn't want Nellie to get married and leave home. But he couldn't bear to have Simon say mean things about her.

"Nellie's pretty. She could have boy-friends if she wanted," he muttered.

"Haw!" mocked Simon. He spat on the ground. "What about the old hag, your grandma? People say she's a witch. Is that right, Willie?"

Tears of fury smarted Willie's eyes. He was afraid if he said anything more, he would blubber. He heard men's voices behind them and suddenly, he turned and dashed back.

"Can I walk with you, please?" he begged, breathlessly.

Both men stopped and peered down at him. They were strangers.

"Sure. Why not? Why, you're only a bairn! Are you workin' in the pit?"

Willie swallowed a lump in his throat. "I'm eleven years old. I'm workin' as a trapper. Started yesterday."

"Right enough. Come along, then."

The men carried on with their conversation. Willie managed to walk between them. He felt safe. He knew as soon as he reached the lamp house Simon wouldn't bother him with so many men around.

He saw no more of Simon that day or the next, and then it was Sunday. He went to church in the morning, as always, but as soon as the service was over, he hurried off to the waterfront to look for Gem.

When he got to the top of the hill and looked down, he saw that the paddock was empty. All the horses were gone. Gem was somewhere in the coal mine.

Willie walked home slowly, kicking at stones along the way. Even when he got home and was told that his father was improving, he was too sad to say anything. He wouldn't talk about his wonderful day at the farm with Charley. He moped around until it was time to go to bed.

The next day when Ned Hall came through the trap, he asked him, "Is it hard to find a horse in a coal mine?"

"No. It's easy as pie," said Ned. "All horses go to the stable when their shift is over. Each stall has the horse's name posted on a board. They get to know their own stall. Sometimes, I don't go to the stable with Sparky. I just unhitch him and he trots off by himself. He wants his supper."

"Oh," said Willie. "Sometime...sometime...could I go to the stable with you?"

"Sure. I'll take you tonight," said Ned.

That night, on their way to the stable, Willie told Ned the whole story of how he had made friends with the little Sable Island mare. He told about how he had hidden in Charley's barn and then had to take Gem back.

"I guess she'll never get out of the mine again," mourned Willie.

"Not if she makes a good pit pony," said Ned, cheerfully.

"What if she doesn't? What if she can't be trained to work like Sparky?"

Ned shook his head sadly.

"Usually a horse like that has to be destroyed. If it can't be trained, it probably won't get sold outside. Nobody wants a kicker or a biter."

"Gem ain't lazy. She wouldn't ever kick or bite," said Willie.

"That's all right, then," said Ned, grinning.

The dimly lighted stables seemed brighter than any other part of the mine. The rough stone walls and pit props had been freshly whitewashed. A strong, horsy smell filled Willie's nostrils. He might have been in one of the livery stables in town. It was the kind of place he loved.

Each animal had its own stall and on each overhead beam was a name—NELLIE, CLYDE, MOLLY—Willie walked the length of the stable, reading each name aloud, until he came to the very end.

GEM.

It really was Gem, with the white blaze on her nose, her long blond mane prettily combed, and her thick, woolly coat beginning to look smooth and neat.

She looked around at him, showing the whites of her eyes, and giving a whicker of recognition.

"Gem!" cried Willie. He buried his face in her soft, warm neck.

For a long time, Willie stayed in the stable with Gem patting her and talking to her.

"Ah, you have new shoes, Gem...very nice...and you're goin' to have a fine new harness. You'll have a leather cap to wear on your head...and pretty brass studs on your face mask. You'll look pretty, Gem...."

He looked around to see Ned watching him.

"It's Gem! She's my horse," said Willie.

"Well, good. Have a visit, then. I spoke to the stableman and he don't mind if you stay for awhile."

Willie was anxious. "Has Gem started to work yet?"

Ned shook his head. "She's been a bit fractious. She was fine above ground but now she's wary of the dark tunnels."

Willie's eyes grew wide with fear. "What's goin' to happen to her then?"

"I dunno. It depends if they can find a driver who can handle her."

"I could handle her!" cried Willie.

Ned rolled the cud of tobacco in his mouth and spat on the ground.

"I'll speak to the stableman and we'll talk about it tomorrow. Good night, Willie."

Willie was filled with a wild hope. His heart pounded so hard, it hurt. He forgot how tired he was. He ran all the way home and told John what Ned had said.

"I might be goin' to be a driver," he

shouted with happiness.

John looked worried. "Calm down, Willie. Your friend, Ned, shouldn't get your hopes up like that. It's not likely they'll let a little boy like you drive a wild horse."

"But she's not really wild," said Willie.

"Lots of men have been killed or injured, drivin'," said John. "Sometimes there's a runaway box, if it's not properly spragged. Sometimes a box goes off the rails and upsets. Sometimes a horse. . . ."

"I don't care," interrupted Willie. "I'll be a good driver if they'll just give me a chance. You wait and see!"

CHAPTER 7

The very next day, the overman arrived at Willie's trap with another boy to take his place.

"Next time Ned Hall comes through, you get on the box with him. Ned will teach you a few things about driving," said the overman.

Willie couldn't believe his luck. What a good friend Ned Hall had turned out to be!

Ned came along, and he and Willie sat together on the box.

"Gem will work in very low seams," Ned explained. "Some are only about one metre high. Just a couple of miners work at the face, pickin' coal. They'll do the loading. Sometimes it's so low they have to work on their hands and knees. There's just barely enough room to get the coal tossed in between the roof and the top of the box."

"Sounds like a tight squeeze," said Willie.

Ned agreed. "If you get the job, all you'd have to do would be to drive back and forth as fast as you safely can. The men depend on you to get the coal out. But you'd have to be very careful. You wouldn't want Gem to stumble on the rough roadway. You wouldn't want her to scrape her head or shoulders on the ceiling or the sides. Drivin' isn't as simple as trappin', Willie b'y."

"But it's a lot more fun," said Willie.

"Fun!" said Ned, laughing. "I never thought of it as bein' fun. But I like my work. Now if you was drivin', when you get out to the landing you would unhitch Gem from the full box. Then you'd hitch onto an empty. Then back you go, back and forth, back and forth, all day long. D'you think that would be fun?"

"I know I'd like it," insisted Willie.

That night they walked home together. Willie learned that Ned boarded at a house on Monkey Row. Ned was unmarried and had come from Newfoundland three years before.

All that week, Willie worked with Ned, driving back and forth, getting to know all the hazards of driving, and all the duties of a driver.

The weekend came, and after church

Nellie and Willie walked two kilometres to the hospital to see their father. He was thin and pale and bearded. One leg was attached to a pulley which raised his leg from the bed.

He smiled at his children. "So now you're the man of the house, Willie," he said.

Willie smiled at him shyly. "Yes, Papa. I'll get my pay at the end of the month. Halloween night," he said.

"Good boy. I can remember when I got my first bobtail sheet," said his father. He tried to change his position, and winced with pain.

"I'm goin' to try out as a driver soon," said Willie. He couldn't keep the hope out of his voice. "Maybe I'll get a raise!" But he thought he'd better not mention that, if he got the job, he would be driving Gem, a Sable Island horse.

"A driver!" His father was surprised. "Maybe all that time you spent at the stables wasn't a waste, after all."

Before Willie could reply, a nurse came and told them they should go.

Nellie kissed her father. "We'll come next Sunday, if we can," she promised.

"Good," said her father. He gave a little moan of pain and closed his eyes. When they got outside, Willie asked, "Do you really think Pa will get better?"

"Yes, I do. And he's so pleased and proud you went to work," said Nellie.

Willie didn't say anything. If he could get to be a driver, maybe he would work until Christmas and go back to school in January. Maybe he wouldn't miss his grade. He could study hard and catch up.

When Willie and Nellie arrived at Sunny Row, they saw a horse and wagon tethered to the hitching post at the entry of the lane. Willie stopped short.

"That mare looks like old Topsy," he exclaimed. He ran over to the black horse with the sway back and rubbed her nose. "Yes, it really is Topsy!" he shouted with joy.

He ran ahead and burst into the kitchen. There was Charley, sitting on the couch next to the warm stove, talking to Grandma as if he'd known her all his life. Grandma was laughing. Grandma hadn't laughed since the day of the accident.

Before Willie could say hello, Sara came bouncing up to him with a big, orange pumpkin in her arms.

"Look, Willie, look! Mister Charley gave us some pumpkins! Now me and you and Maggie can make pumpkin grinners for Halloween! I never had a pumpkin grinner before in my whole life!"

Grandma spoke up from her rocking chair. "Hush, Sara. Remember it is the Sabbath Day."

Sara said, "Yes, today is the Sabbath but tomorrow is Monday, and it's Halloween. We can make grinners as soon as we get home from school, can't we, Grandma? We know how to do it, don't we, Maggie?"

"Yes, but we have to let Nellie cut the cover around the stem," said Maggie in her quiet way. She hugged her pumpkin. Her smile was almost as wide as Sara's.

"Then you take a big spoon and take out all the insides," said Sara.

John, who had his leg in its wooden splints propped up on a chair, grinned at them. "And then you give Nellie all the insides to make pumpkin pie. And then you give me all the seeds to roast in the oven," he teased.

Everybody laughed.

Nellie took off her coat and hung it on a peg. "Won't you stay for supper?" she invited Charley.

"Thanks, but I have to get home before dark," he said. "I just wanted to stay long enough to see Willie. How are you making out in the mine, lad?"

"It's all right," said Willie. "I get paid tomorrow. Then Grandma can have tea."

"Good boy," said Charley.

"And I'm gettin' a chance to try out as a driver. Gem is down there. I might get a chance to drive her."

"That's just great!" exclaimed Charley as he picked up his cap to take his departure.

"Please come back. I want to have a real visit with you," begged Willie.

"Thank you. I'll have to get permission from my cranky sister first," said Charley, chuckling as he went out the door.

Each night now, Willie borrowed the tin alarm clock from Nellie. He asked her to make up his lunch before she went to bed. By getting up very early, he hoped to avoid Simon on his way to work.

The only heat in the house came from the coal-burning stove in the kitchen. Overnight, the fire went out. In winter sometimes, even the water in the tea-kettle froze solid.

On the last day in October, Willie shivered with cold as he crawled out of bed. John still had to sleep downstairs in the parlour. Willie lit his candle and crept down the steep, narrow stair. He gobbled a bowl of cold oatmeal porridge and went out into the dark morning. He hurried along by himself, whistling to keep up his courage. No one else was on the path.

At the lamp house he exchanged his tag for a lantern, then stopped at the deputy's cabin underground where he was told to go back to his trap. He was disappointed. He would not have a driving lesson that day. Maybe they had decided he couldn't be a driver, after all.

He had plenty of time to visit Gem, anyway, before he went to his trap. He found his way along the dark passages to the stable.

The short, stocky stableman, called "Stubby," nodded at him.

"You can give Gem her breakfast, if you like," he said.

He showed Willie how to measure the grain.

"A new seam has been opened. A small, narrow one. They'll be wanting a pony or a small horse. If Gem's harness is finished, and if Ned Hall says you're ready, you can try out as a driver, soon," said Stubby.

Willie jumped for joy. He whistled merrily as he went about his chores, feeding Gem and brushing down her coat. It seemed like this Halloween day might turn out to be one of the happiest days of his life.

The long hours passed at the trap and when at last the shift was over, Willie found himself standing in line at the office with other miners to receive his first pay envelope and his "bobtail sheet." It was called a bobtail sheet because with the cash was a statement. The company deducted the cost of rent, coal, medical fees, and even church collections from each miner's pay. Many miners did not get any cash because they were deeply in debt to the Company Store. All they got was a bobtail sheet, stating how much they owed.

But Willie's envelope contained some cash. It was a proud moment.

He counted the money. Two dollars and forty-seven cents. How much could Nellie buy with that? The flour was getting low in the barrel. There was hardly any kerosene for the lamp, and Grandma was longing for a cup of tea.

As he limped out of the line-up, Willie wiggled his big toe. It was sticking out of the end of his right boot. There was a hole in the bottom of his left boot. He had a sore on the sole of this foot, making him limp.

But he couldn't hope for new boots this month. Food was more important.

Carefully, he put the money and the bobtail sheet into his piece-can, as all the men did, in order to keep it clean from the coal dust which blackened their hands and clothes.

Willie was one of the last to leave the office because he had visited Gem again before he went up on the rake. Outside he discovered a light snowfall had covered the ground, and a cold wind was blowing. Ahead he saw some strange lights bobbing around. There was a sound of distant shouting.

Halloween! Pranksters would be abroad. He'd better hurry home.

He shivered and tried to run to keep himself warm, limping on his sore foot. When he came to the graveyard, he could see tombstones gleaming like pale ghosts in the wintry night.

It had almost stopped snowing, and he decided he could see the way well enough to take a shortcut through the cemetery. He whistled under his breath as he picked his way along the path.

A low moan came from behind one of the tombstones. He stopped and listened. Again he heard a moan, as if someone was

in pain. He couldn't be sure because of the sighing of the wind in the trees overhead.

"Who's there?" he asked.

No one answered.

He started on again, his heart pounding. He wished he hadn't taken the shortcut. Maybe he was imagining things. Then he saw something white floating between the trees and the tombstones.

He decided to go back, but when he turned to go he saw another ghostly form with a light. He stood still, too scared to move in either direction.

A violent push sent him sprawling to the ground. His piece-can was snatched from his hand. As he struggled to his feet, he heard someone laugh.

"Run for it, Smarty Pants!" a jeering voice shouted.

He knew that voice. Simon Ross!

He and his pals had stolen the piece-can, with all Willie's money.

CHAPTER 8

When Willie reached the safety of his own back porch he stood for a moment in the dark, trying to gain control of himself. His whole body was trembling. He would have to tell his family he had lost his money and John's piece-can.

Inside, all was quiet except for the soft drone of his grandmother's voice. He opened the door.

Two pumpkin grinners sat on the table, their orange bodies and funny faces aglow with the light of the candles inside. They cast spooky shadows on the walls and ceilings. The air was scented with the exotic smell of the lighted pumpkins and something spicy Nellie was stirring in a pot on the stove. John was sitting with his injured leg propped up on a chair, and the two little girls were on the floor, snuggled up to their grandmother in her rocking chair. She was telling them a story. . . .

Tap! Tap! The knock came again on the door. *The eve was so wild and stormy no* human being should have been abroad. That burly Scotsman was afraid to open the door. But open it he did. He looked down. He saw nothing but a little wet and bedraggled brown hen.

"Let me in, for the love of God," said the hen.

The dog by the fireplace gave a low growl. The hackles rose on its neck. . . .

Grandmother's story stopped as she saw Willie at the door. "Oh, here's the man of the house come home with his first pay envelope."

"No," said Willie. "No, Grandma." He wished his voice wouldn't tremble as he spoke.

The whole family chorused in unison, "Why? What happened?"

"It was stolen," said Willie. He bit his lip to keep from crying.

John grabbed his crutches and got up from his chair. "Stolen! Tell us what happened."

Willie blurted out the story of the attack in the graveyard.

"It was Simon Ross. I know it was. I heard his laugh."

John was furious. "Wait until I get this splint off my leg! I'll make him be sorry."

Willie threw himself down on a chair.

"I worked all those days for nothin'! I ain't got a cent!" he mourned.

Nellie helped him off with his dusty sweater and overalls and tried to comfort him.

"Maybe you haven't got any actual money, Willie, but did you look at your bobtail sheet? Because you worked, the rent for this house is paid for—a dollar fifty for the month. Fifty cents for coal, fifteen cents for school, forty cents for the doctor, and ten cents for church. All those things. . . ."

"Wait a minute!" John interrupted. "Pa and I worked the first part of the month. Did they give you our pay, too?"

Willie's face brightened. "No. I forgot to ask."

"We can collect that. There should be enough for flour and tea."

"What about Willie's new boots?" asked Maggie.

"Why don't he charge them at the Company Store? Everybody else does," said Sara.

"No," said Grandma firmly. "Everybody does except us. We don't charge. We make do without."

Everyone was silent.

Then Nellie said, "Better get scrubbed,

Willie. There's pumpkin pie for your supper."

The two little girls put their pigtailed heads against their grandmother's knees.

"Please finish the story, Grandma," begged Maggie.

"Oh, well, you know that story. I've told it to ye many a time," said Grandma, in a tired voice. She needed her cup of tea.

"But we want to hear it again," said Sara, and her grandmother sighed and continued.

The hen came in and warmed herself by the fire. As she preened her feathers she began to grow.

"Bigger and bigger and bigger...." the girls chanted with her.

"Yes!" *Bigger and bigger until she was as big as the farmer himself. He was very afraid. He opened the door to the wild storm.*

"Get out!" he shouted to the big hen.

The hen scuttled out of the door. The dog sprang to its feet and took after her. The man could hear the dog barking and the hen squawking outside.

The next day the doctor was called to tend an old woman in the village who had been mauled by a dog.

"And that's the end of the story."

"Not really," said Maggie.

"Because after that, everybody knew the old woman was a witch," said Sara.

Her grandmother smiled and patted her rosy cheek. "That's not in the story. Blow out your candles in your pumpkins. We can't waste any more. Anyway, it's time wee bairns were in bed."

Maggie sighed. "This would have been the very happiest Halloween in my life if it wasn't for mean Simon Ross," she said.

"I hate Simon! I hope John beats him to pieces," said Sara, fiercely.

"All right now. We won't say anything more about it," said Nellie as Willie came out of the pantry, scrubbed and clean. "Don't you worry. Everything will be all right."

Willie sat down to eat. The pumpkin pie was delicious, but he knew everything wouldn't be all right. Not until John was able to beat up Simon. He wished he was big enough and strong enough to do it himself, but he knew it would be ridiculous for him to try.

He had never hated anybody as much as he hated Simon Ross.

He managed to avoid him the rest of the week. For the next three days he continued to work with Ned and Sparky, but on Thursday he was told to go back to his trap. He was in despair. He thought he had failed the driver's test, but he was afraid to ask Stubby. The stableman still let Willie give Gem her oats and have a visit with her each night.

On Sunday, Willie's foot was so sore he couldn't go to church. Nellie took Maggie and Sara to see their father in the hospital. They brought back the good news that he was much improved.

"He'll be home for Christmas," said Nellie, happily.

Willie was glad, but he had to ask, "Will he be able to work again?"

"Maybe not as a hand-pick miner, but he'll get a job above ground, eventually," Nellie assured him.

Willie was quiet. What did she mean by "eventually"?

He was soaking his foot in a pan of hot water and creolin, the only disinfectant they had. It smelled strong and clean. John was trying to mend Willie's worn-out boot by making an insole from an old piece of leather Sara had found discarded in a ditch.

Sara often found things in ditches. Sometimes they could be put to good use.

"But you'll have to throw away that

broken china cup. It's no earthly good for anything. We have no room for trash," said Grandma, looking up from her rocking chair.

"It's so pretty! It has a pink rose in the corner," Sara protested, holding it up to show her.

Grandma sniffed. She was not in a good mood. She did not approve of John working on Sunday, like a cobbler.

" 'Remember the Sabbath Day to keep it holy,' " she quoted from the Bible.

"It's the only day I can do it. Willie has to wear the boots tomorrow," said John.

Just then a knock sounded at the door.

"Maybe it's Charley!" exclaimed Willie, jerking his foot out of the pan of disinfectant.

But it was not Charley.

At first, Willie didn't recognize the man with his face freshly scrubbed and shaved. He had a short, straight nose, sparkling hazel eyes, and a wide smile. He pulled off his cap and bowed to Grandma.

As soon as he said, "Good day, Ma'am," Willie knew who it was.

"It's Ned! Ned Hall! Come in and meet my family."

Ned nodded and smiled shyly at each one. He accepted the chair Nellie offered.

"I've come to bring you good news, Willie," he said. He turned his cap around and around in his strong hands. "You are to go to the stable first thing in the morning. You are to take Gem into the new seam."

Willie gave a loud whistle. He hopped all around the room on his good foot, uttering little squeaks of joy.

The girls giggled, but John asked anxiously, "Do you really think he can handle that horse?"

Ned nodded. "Yes. He's got a way with her. Seems like he's been around horses all his life." He looked down at the floor, holding his cap between his knees. "He'll get a rise in pay, too. I know you got trouble here."

"I'll be back to work in a month," said John, proudly. He gave the children a warning look. They understood they were not to say anything about Willie being robbed of his pay.

"Won't you stay for supper?" Nellie invited.

"Thank you, Miss," said Ned.

Willie noticed he kept glancing at Nellie and she looked back at him under her eyelashes in a funny sort of way.

The little girls liked Ned. He fitted into

the family as if they had always known him. Willie was so happy he couldn't stop smiling and laughing. He was sorry when Ned said good night, but he couldn't wait for Monday morning.

Gem seemed to be waiting for him. Maybe she was glad to go to work. Stubby helped Willie fasten on the new harness. A thick leather cap fitted over her head and a flap decorated with shiny brass studs came down over her nose.

"The head is the tallest part of an animal and most likely to get bumped and injured," the stableman explained. "But this here critter ain't so likely to bump her head as her sides. All them Sable Island ponies have swollen bellies. It's from the coarse marram grass they et when they was wild." He slapped Gem's belly. "This one is so swole you'd think she was goin' to have a baby." He snorted with laughter and Willie felt offended.

"Ned says she'll be a better shape soon, eating oats and hay and working every day," he said defensively.

"Off you go then," said Stubby.

Willie was on his own.

He took Gem out to the landing and was shown an empty box to hitch to her traces. Then he was given directions to find the coal seam where he would be working. He led Gem by her bridle, talking and whistling to her as they went along the dark passageways.

The new seam was very narrow, very rough, low ceilinged, and dark. The only light came from Willie's clanny lamp. He thought how terrible it would be if his light went out. But he was proud, very proud, and happy to be working alone with his own horse in the coal mine. Not many boys of eleven would be given such a responsibility.

There was only one trap in this new seam. The boy who opened the door was tall and thin, and had a cough. Willie could hear him coughing before he reached the door.

"You sound like you've got a bad cold," said Willie.

"I ain't got a cold. I cough all the time. It's gettin' worse. Ma says it's the gallopin' consumption."

Willie was shocked. He knew anyone who had consumption would die.

"You should be home in bed," he said.

"My Pa won't let me," said the boy. He coughed again and spit a mouthful of blood on the ground.

The next day, in the stable, Stubby told

Willie that the boy could no longer work. Another trapper had taken his place. Willie didn't know who it was until he and Gem reached the trap.

Simon Ross was grinning from ear to ear when he opened the door.

"Glad you whistle all the time, Wee Willie. I'll always know when you're a-comin'."

Willie didn't answer.

He had been so happy, driving Gem. The Sable Island horse had proved a willing worker and had caused no trouble at all. The colliers at the workplace had praised both Willie and Gem.

"A good team," they had said.

Now everything was spoiled.

The next time Willie came through the trap, Gem stumbled on a pile of rocks. The rocks had not been there before.

"Whoa," said Willie. He examined Gem's foot to make sure she had not been lamed. He picked up the rocks and cleared the path. He knew Simon had put them there, but he didn't say anything.

He thought Simon wouldn't dare to do anything really dangerous. He knew the rules. When he had taken Willie around on his first working day, Simon had said, "Every man's life depends on the life of another in the pits."

That night, Willie met Ned Hall when he took Gem to the stable. They walked back together. On the way, Willie said nothing about Simon, but Ned asked a lot of questions about Nellie.

Finally Willie asked, "Are you sweet on her?"

Ned laughed. "Tell you the truth, Willie, she seems like the nicest girl I ever met."

"She is," said Willie. Somehow he didn't mind that Ned was sweet on her.

"You better come in," he invited, when they got to Sunny Row.

"Can't. Not in these dirty pit clothes. But I'll come over some evenin' soon," Ned promised.

And he kept his promise the very next night.

Since he had become a driver, Willie had formed the habit of hanging his piece-can on a spike on one of the pit props, not far from the trap. That night, when Nellie opened the can to wash it, a live rat jumped out.

Nellie screamed.

"It wasn't me!" cried Willie.

There was a wild scramble. Grandma crawled up on the couch, and Nellie stood

on a chair, holding tight to her skirts. The little girls laughed hysterically. Ned was laughing, too. John managed to stun the rat with one of his crutches, and then Ned caught it and threw it out the back door.

"Now who would play a trick like that on you, Willie?" he asked.

Willie and John exchanged glances. They knew very well who had done it, but John said, "I guess it's a joke that's often played on new boys."

Willie knew that as long as Simon remained at the trap, his life would be made miserable. But he didn't want to say anything to any of the miners. John warned him not to get the name of being a whiner and a complainer.

But Willie no longer whistled as he worked. Gem noticed the difference in her young master and often turned her head to look at him.

She, too, worked less willingly now.

And that was the way things were on the day of the explosion.

CHAPTER 9

Wee Willie Maclean had worked as a driver in the Ocean Deeps Mine for nearly a month before the day of the explosion on Level Five. By this time, many of the colliers knew about the small boy and the Sable Island horse. It was said the two worked so well together they could get out as much coal in a day as a full-sized team.

A story was told about another driver, Fibber Foster, who had tried to make Gem work an extra shift one night when his own pit pony went lame. The little mare balked and kicked and refused to enter the tunnel. When Fibber brought Gem back, sweating and bleeding from the cut of a whip, Stubby, the stableman, refused to let him have another horse. Fibber had to go home and lose a night's work.

The next day, Gem worked as willingly as ever for Wee Willie. By now the two were used to working in the mine. With Gem as his companion, Willie often forgot his fears and worries. The only unhappy time was when he went through the trap. Simon was sure to say something hateful or play some small, mean trick. It got so bad that when Willie said his prayers at night he prayed for something to happen so Simon would no longer be working at his trap.

But he hadn't meant anything as bad as an explosion.

On the afternoon of November 28, 1902, Willie was whistling cheerfully as he and Gem headed into the tunnel for the last load of coal for that shift. They were partway to the coal face when Gem suddenly stopped.

"Hey! What's up?" said Willie.

A deep grumble seemed to come from the ground. Then came a great blast of air. Rocks and dust, and pieces of wood flew past. Something hit him, and he was knocked to the ground.

By the time he struggled to his feet, he heard the sound of pounding feet. Men came running.

"C'mon, lad! Leave the horse. Get out of here!"

Stunned and bewildered, Willie hesitated.

He couldn't leave Gem!

She was helpless, caught between the shafts of the box. She was headed in the wrong direction. There was no room to turn her around. She tried to rear up on her hind legs, and screamed with terror.

"Easy, girl, easy!" coaxed Willie, as he put out his light.

The air was so filled with debris he hadn't been able to see much. Now it was pitch dark. He felt as if he was choking to death. Was the air filled with poisonous gas as well?

He had to get out...but he couldn't leave Gem.

Could he make her back up, all the way back to the landing?

A weird silence had followed the explosion. As he struggled to make the terrified horse back up, a faint cry came from far back in the tunnel.

"Help! Help!"

Willie froze.

Simon.

He must be dreaming.

But no one else could be back there, still. The men at the coal face had run for their lives.

The cry came again, desperate, pitiful.

"Help!"

For one terrible moment, Willie

thought he would not...could not...go back. All the pit props, and walls, and ceilings in the tunnel must have been loosened by the explosion. At any moment there might be a rock fall somewhere which would cut off all hope of escape. If he could make Gem back up now, all the way back to the landing, they both could live. Why should they die trying to rescue Simon?

But then, Willie knew he had to go back. Words echoed in his mind. *In the mine every man's life depends on the other.*

He choked out, "Whoa, Gem. Wait. I'll be back."

But even as he said it he thought he never would.

Gem trusted him. He felt her body trembling under his hand, but she had stopped squealing. Maybe she would wait. Maybe she would be all right.

On his hands and knees in the black dark, he felt for one of the steel rails. He began to crawl back farther into the tunnel. His breath came in painful gasps. He tried to yell, "I'm coming!" but his mouth and nose were so full of dust his voice came out as a low croak.

He could no longer hear Simon calling.

Probably he was dead. Still Willie crawled on.

He heard again, "Help!" but the call was weaker now.

"Hold on! I'm coming!" Willie croaked.

At last the rail under his hand ended. He had come to a great pile of rubble.

"Simon! Where are you?"

"I'm caught. I'm buried under the rocks." The sobbing voice was almost in his ear.

"I'll get you out," said Willie.

He felt around with his hands until he touched something soft and furry. It was Simon's head.

He found rocks piled on Simon's left leg and arm which were pinning him down.

"Ow! Ow!" Simon kept howling as Willie pulled and lifted blindly.

"I think you're free. Can you crawl?" Willie asked.

He felt so tired and weak, he wondered if he could crawl back himself.

"I can't...I can't do anything. I think my arm...my shoulder...is broke."

"You've gotta crawl," said Willie. Somehow Simon's moans made him feel stronger. "We gotta get out of here. There might be a cave in any minute. Keep your good hand on the rail."

"O.K. I'll try," sobbed Simon.

It seemed to Willie they had been crawling forever when Simon suddenly whimpered, "I can't go no further."

"You've got to," croaked Willie, desperately.

No answer.

He felt around in the dark. Simon was lying flat on the ground. His body was limp.

He must have passed out.

Willie gave way to despair. He lay beside Simon on the ground. He couldn't get up. He thought he would never move again.

Then he heard a sound. He lifted his head. It came again—a long, shrill whinny.

"Gem!" cried Willie.

In answer, he heard the creaking of harness and the sound of wheels moving along the rail.

The little mare was coming to him.

"Gem!" He sobbed aloud with love and hope as he managed to get on his feet.

He had an idea. If Gem came close, maybe he could get Simon into the empty box...somehow...and maybe Gem would back up...and keep on backing....

She was close to him now.

Oh, if only Simon would wake up.

"Come on, Si! Come on!"

"Ow!" moaned Simon.

"Si, if you can get into the box, Gem can take us out of here."

"O.K.," said Simon. He was getting to his feet.

Willie felt a stab of anger. He thought Simon had been pretending to be unconscious. But somehow, in the dark and narrow space, he managed to help get him into the box.

He felt his way back along Gem's body and found her bridle.

With a great surge of hope he gave the command. "Now back up, girl. Back!"

At that moment another deep rumble came from far back in the tunnel. Again came the sound of falling rocks—this time much nearer. Another rockfall....

Something hit Willie on the head. He heard and felt no more.

CHAPTER 10

Many hours passed before Willie became fully conscious. He found himself on the couch beside the warm kitchen stove. A strand of Nellie's long hair tickled his face. He looked up into her anxious blue eyes.

"Where's Gem?" he whispered.

"Shhh! Be still. Don't worry."

"How did I get home?"

"Ned found you. You're a hero, Willie. They say you saved Simon Ross's life."

"Is he hurt bad?"

"He has a bruised shoulder and a broken arm. But they got Simon out first. He didn't breathe as much afterdamp as you did, Willie. And you had a concussion. Now rest."

Nellie left him but Maggie and Sara came, in their white, flour bag night gowns, their long hair flowing loose.

"Mrs. Ross sent you some cookies," said Maggie.

Sara screwed up her little face.

"Yuck! They taste awful," she said.

"Now, now," said Grandma from her rocking chair.

John hobbled over. "What's it feel like to be a hero, Willie?"

"It feels awful," he said.

They all laughed.

"Say good night now, girls," said Nellie. "You should have been in bed long ago."

The next morning, after the children had left for school, Willie and John and Nellie sat at the kitchen table for a late breakfast. Outside the window, big snowflakes drifted down.

Willie was feeling much better. He was telling all he could remember about what had happened at the time of the explosion, when a knock came at the door.

It was Simon.

His round face was pale, and his arm was in a sling. He stamped snow from his boots on the hooked rug at the door before he shuffled over to Willie.

"I come to say thank ya for savin' me," he said.

Willie grinned. Simon sounded as if he was reciting a lesson at school.

"That's all right, Si. Anyone would've done the same," he said.

But in his mind, he remembered how close he had come to not going back for the boy who had bullied him.

Simon brought his good hand out from behind his back. He held out John's piece-can.

"I found this in...er...the cemetery. Looked like it might be yours."

"Oh, good!" exclaimed Willie. "Did you look inside? Was there any money?"

Simon's face turned red. "Naw. I didn't find no money," he mumbled.

Willie knew Simon had spent it. "Well, thanks for the can," he said.

Nellie was always kind. "Won't you sit down?" she invited.

"Naw. I better go home. I jus' wanted ya to know, Willie."

"That's all right, Si," said Willie, again.

When Simon had gone, John said, "I suppose you and Simon will be great friends, now."

Willie laughed. "You s'pose wrong. But you won't have to beat him up now, John. He won't bother me no more."

"I bet he won't," said John.

Willie pushed his porridge bowl away. "I wish't I could see Gem," he said.

"You couldn't go down, even if you were well. The mine is always closed for at least three days after an explosion. They have to make sure it's safe," said John.

Willie stood up. He still felt dizzy and weak. He went over to the couch to lie down, just as another knock came on the door.

This time it was Ned Hall. He shook snow from his cap and hung it on a peg. He gave Nellie his wide smile. Then he drew up a chair beside Willie.

"How're you feelin', b'y?"

"Fine," said Willie.

"I've got some big news for you, Willie. Think you can stand it?"

"What is it?"

"Some of it is good—and some of it is very bad."

"Is it about Gem?"

Ned's face was sad. "Yes, b'y."

Willie thought his heart would stop beating. "Is she dead?"

Ned nodded. "She didn't survive the accident, Willie. She was crushed in the rock fall. But she was a great horse. I think she saved your life, and Simon's, too."

Willie gave a great cry. "She's dead! Why couldn't I die, too? I want to be dead!"

"No," said Ned. With one big, hard

hand he pushed Willie back on the couch. "Listen to me, b'y. Listen, Willie. I have some good news."

Willie put his hands over his ears. Tears streamed down his face. "Nothin' is good! I don't want to hear it!"

Ned pulled one of Willie's hands away. "Yes, you do, Willie. Because, in a way, Gem ain't dead. Somethin' wonderful happened last night. Somethin' that never happened in the Ocean Deeps Mine before."

Willie shut his eyes and lay back, sobbing. Ned kept on talking.

"Remember how Stubby teased you about Gem's fat belly? He feels some foolish now! He never guessed, but Gem really was pregnant. She lived long enough to give birth, after we dug her out."

Nellie came over to the couch to comfort Willie. She lifted his head against her shoulder. "Do you mean Gem had a baby? Honest?" she asked.

"Yes. There's a wee, live foal. He looks all the world like his mother. Same colour. Same blaze on his nose."

Willie said, "I don't b'lieve you."

"It's true, Willie. In a few days you'll see the foal for yourself."

Willie stared at him. His body still shuddered with the last of his sobs. He couldn't sort out his thoughts.

After a while he said, "Gem's baby.... What will happen to the foal?"

Ned patted Willie's shoulder. "Well... that I don't know. It belongs to the Company, a'course. You get better fast, and we'll go down to see him in a few days."

Nellie said, "You go to sleep now, Willie. Doctor's orders."

Ned pushed back his chair, and Nellie covered her brother with an old afghan.

"Try not to grieve, Willie," she said. "Try not to think about Gem. Think about the little foal, instead."

"I don't want that foal to grow up to be a pit pony," Willie murmured.

He closed his eyes.

From her rocking chair, his grandmother began to sing an old Gaelic lullaby. Nellie put her flatirons on the stove to heat and began to sort and fold clean laundry. John and Ned sat at the table and sorted dry beans for baking. They talked together in low voices. The room was warm and safe and comfortable. Willie fell asleep.

When he awakened, the little girls had come home from school. They were talking about Gem's foal.

"It has to have a name. I think Gem's baby should be called 'Jewel,'" said Maggie.

"No. That would be a funny name for a boy horse," protested Sara.

"Gem came from Sable Island," said Ned. "Maybe you could call it 'Sable.'"

Willie sat up. "'Sable' is the French word for 'sand,'" he said. "I like that. We could call it 'Sandy.'" Then he flopped back on his pillow, and added, angrily, "What's the sense of talkin' about a name? The foal will live all its life in the pits. You girls will never see it."

Into his mind's eye came the picture of the newborn foals he had seen in the Green Bay stables. He could see them struggling up to balance themselves on their wobbly new legs, nudging their mothers, looking for milk.

"Gem is dead! How can the foal live without any milk from its mother?" he cried.

"They'll use a baby's nursing bottle. Didn't you know that?" said Sara.

"Right," said Ned. "The foal will be all right, don't you worry. And maybe it won't stay in the mine. Some say, now, that machinery can do the work of horses.

Some day, there won't be no horses in mines."

Willie sat up again. "Is that true?" he demanded.

John answered, "Yes. I've heard a lot of talk about electric power and new kinds of machinery."

Willie tried to imagine what a mine would be like without horses. "Won't they need people, neither?"

Both men laughed. "Ya hafta have people to run the machinery, b'y. There'll always be colliers. But the work will be different, that's for sure."

Nellie said, "Anyway, it hasn't happened yet."

She folded the last flour bag pillowcase.

"It's time for supper. Think you can come to the table for some fried potatoes, Willie?"

"Oh, we forgot to tell you," said John. "Ned's goin' to stay here. I mean—he's going to be our boarder. That's if you don't mind sleepin' on a straw mat on the hall floor."

Willie's face brightened. "A boarder? He's gonna stay here? A'course I don't mind!"

And he discovered, in spite of his grief,

he was able to eat two helpings of fried potatoes.

Late in the afternoon of the next day, Ned moved in. Along with his few belongings he brought two codfish heads. Nellie made *ceann groppaig* for supper, to celebrate.

Maggie and Sara had just finished washing the dishes, and John had turned down the lamp wick to save kerosene when there was a sudden great commotion outside in the street. Bells jangled and people shouted. Then came a loud, horrible, rattling sound.

Maggie and Sara rushed to the window. Grandma got up from her rocking chair.

"It sounds like *Oidhche Na Calluinn*,"* she exclaimed.

"You're right!" said John, peering over the heads of the little girls.

"I wonder who it's for?" said Willie, coming from behind and trying to see.

Maggie was first to guess. "I think it's for us," she said.

Even little Sara knew about the old Scottish custom of bringing food and a blessing to a household in trouble. She listened in solemn wonder with the others, as the parade circled their house

* eye' yuh nuh cal' lin

three times. The horrible rattling sounds were made by people beating on dried sheepskins. The leader, who had a woolly skin pulled over his head for a disguise, stopped at the door and shouted out the words of the *Duan Na Calluinn*.* When he came to the last lines, John opened the door.

Friends and neighbours shouted greetings and jostled each other as they entered the house. Each one brought a gift of food—potatoes and onions, turnips, mutton, and beef. All went into a big canvas bag held open by the leader, whose face was still covered.

When the last gift had been donated, the leader was unmasked.

It was old Charley, with his long, white beard and twinkling, blue eyes.

"Charley! How did you get here?" cried Willie.

"A brownie told me about the *Calluinn*," said Charley. He winked at Ned, and Willie knew who the brownie was.

Already, Freddie the Fiddler was getting out his violin. In a moment, a space was cleared in the middle of the kitchen floor for the dancers and singers and storytellers.

Willie had been at many ceilidhs

* dan' nuh cal' lin

110

before. He always wondered how so many people could get into such a small room and still have space to dance more than one couple at a time. He loved music and soon his toes were tapping. He joined in the singing until someone called out, "Whistle us a tune, Wee Willie Maclean!"

"What shall I whistle, then?"

"Give us a Nova Scotia tune!"

"What shall it be?"

"Give us 'The Braes of Margaree.'"

Willie stood with his hands in his ragged pants pockets, and whistled the lilting tune. Soon voices joined in, singing in Gaelic of the beauties of the Cape Breton countryside in summer, of green meadows and grazing cattle, of birds singing, of men fishing for salmon in the broad rivers. They sang of the companionship of joyful milling-frolics, of parties and of weddings...and when it came to that part, at the end of the song, Willie saw that Ned had his arm around Nellie. He held her close and kissed her.

Willie bowed to his audience and went back to his place. Then old Charley took the floor.

"I have a story to tell," he said.

Everybody listened.

"It's the story of a young lad whose

father and brother were hurt in a mining accident. He was a boy who didn't want to be a miner, but when there was no wage earner in the family he went down into the mine to work as a trapper. This boy had a great love of horses. There was a pit pony in the mine—a Sable Island horse—which he loved above all others. A day came when he was able to be a driver. He was happy to drive the pit pony he loved. Then one day there was a bump—an explosion—in the seam where he worked. He might have run for his life but he heard someone call for help. He went back, and saved another boy's life.

"That night a strange thing happened. His pit pony gave birth to a foal. Although she died soon after the birthing, it was a kind of miracle. Such a thing had never happened in a mine before. What could the Company do with a foal?

"Let me tell you that this boy had many friends. One of his friends was a farmer. He offered to buy the foal and keep it on his farm. But the Company decided to give the foal to the boy, with the understanding that the farmer would agree to keep it on his farm—for the time being."

Old Charley paused. The room was so

quiet, Willie thought everybody could hear his heart pounding for joy.

"Come out on the floor, Wee Willie. I have a paper for you, signed by the Mine Manager. It says the foal—name of 'Sandy'—will be registered in your name."

Willie stepped out, smiling so hard it hurt his face. Charley gave him the paper and a light slap on the back. Everybody clapped.

Then Freddie the Fiddler began to play a farewell tune. People shouted and sang as they prepared to go home. Soon, everyone had gone except Charley. He would sleep on the couch by the stove that night.

"I wish Pa could have been here," said Willie.

"That reminds me," said Charley. "I stopped by to tell your dad about this. You know he'll be home for Christmas. But he sent word that as soon as John goes back to work, you can go back to school, if you want."

Willie looked around for a chair and sat down with a plunk. His mind was in a whirl. He didn't know what to say or think.

"You don't have to decide right now,

Willie. Pa said it's up to you," said John.

"It would seem awful queer to be a kid in school again," said Willie.

Grandma stopped rocking back and forth.

"You're a bright bairn, laddie. You'll be sorry when you get older if you miss the chance to get a wee bit education."

Then Willie remembered his mother's words. *If you study hard you can be anything you want to be. . . .*

He heard Charley say, "And there's Sandy. I'll need somebody to come and help me on the farm during school holidays. I'll need somebody to help me train that colt."

Willie gave a low whistle. "There ain't no choice. Where are my books?" he demanded.

And everybody laughed.

GLOSSARY

bairn (bern):   a child

bobtail sheet: pay envelope containing a statement of deductions from each miner's pay

ceann groppaig (cown' gro' pik):   a codfish head stuffed with rolled oats, flour, and cod livers

ceilidh (kay' lee):   an informal social gathering featuring traditional Scottish or Irish songs and dances

collier (kol' yer):   a coal miner

colliery (kol' yer ee):   a coal mine, its buildings, and equipment

Duan Na Calluinn (dan' nuh cal' lin):   ditty or song sung before a celebration

firedamp: a mixture of poisonous and explosive gases, consisting mainly of methane, which seeps from displaced coal

Gaelic (gay' lik):   the Scottish Highlanders, or their language

Oidhche Na Calluinn (eye' yuh nuh kal' lin): a Scottish custom of bringing food to a household in trouble

pithead: the top of a mine shaft

rake: a string of cars that runs on rails inside a mine

seam: a layer of coal

ABOUT THE AUTHOR

Joyce Barkhouse is a former teacher who lives in Halifax, Nova Scotia. Although she has been writing stories for many years, she was 61 when her first book was published, *George Dawson: The Little Giant* (Natural Heritage). Since then, she has won many awards for excellence in writing. *The Witch of Port LaJoye* (Ragweed Press), was a Children's Book Centre Choice. She intends to keep on writing about the lives of early Canadians. "Everyone should know about their roots," she says. She is planning a book about her early memories of growing up in Nova Scotia which she is sure her grandchildren will enjoy, (she has five) and, of course, plans to write more historical fiction.

Other books in the Jeanpac Series you might want to read:

ACKNOWLEDGMENTS

The author owes a debt of gratitude to many people for their interest and help with this work, especially to her friend and mentor, Janet Lunn; her son-in-law, Greg Howard; her two children, Murray and Janet, as well as to other members of her immediate family.

Thanks, also, to Hope Bridgewater of the Halifax Regional Library, to the staff of the Glace Bay Miners Museum, and to all those miners who shared their knowledge and experiences, including Miles McCabe, William Pittman, and Eddie Pierog.

Thanks, too, for the hospitality and encouragement of her friends, Evelyn and Donald Sutherland of Sydney, Nova Scotia.